THE BUS FOR US

Suzanne Bloom

Boyds Mills Press
Honesdale, Pennsylvania

Boyds Mills Press, Inc.
815 Church Street
Honesdale, Pennsylvania 18431
Printed in China

Library of Congress Cataloging-in-Publication Data

Bloom, Suzanne.
      The bus for us / written and illustrated by Suzanne Bloom.—1st ed.
  [32]p. : col. ill. ; cm.
Summary: On her first day of school, Tess wonders what the school bus
will look like.
 ISBN 978-1-56397-932-3
1. School — Fiction. 2. School buses — Fiction. I. Title.
 [E] 21 2001   AC   CIP
00-102348

First edition
The text of this book is set in 26-point Palatino.

20 19 18 17 16 15 14 13 12 11

To four fabulous first-grade teachers and to Alice, who always asked.
—S. B.

"Is this the bus for us, Gus?"

"No, Tess. This is a taxi."

BUS
STOP

"Is this the bus for us, Gus?"

"No, Tess. This is a tow truck."

"Is this the bus for us, Gus?"

"No, Tess. This is a fire engine."

"Is this the bus for us, Gus?"

"No, Tess. This is an ice-cream truck."

"Is this the bus for us, Gus?"

"No, Tess. This is a garbage truck."

"Is this the bus for us, Gus?"

"No, Tess. This is a backhoe."

"Is this the bus for us, Gus?"

"Yes, Tess. This is the bus for us. Let's go!"

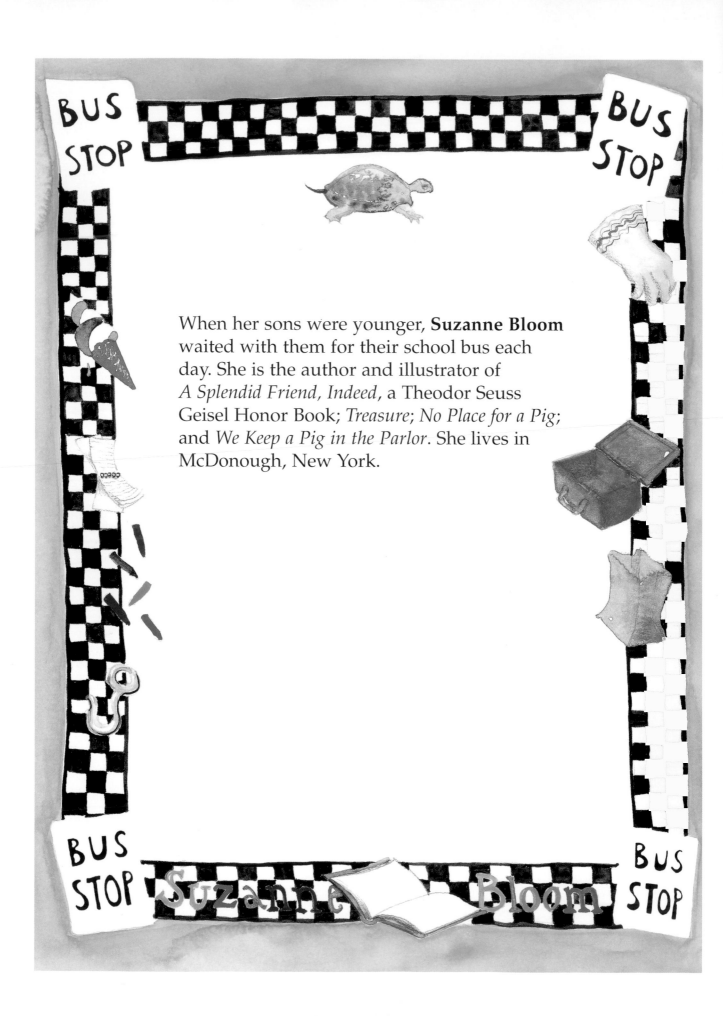

When her sons were younger, **Suzanne Bloom** waited with them for their school bus each day. She is the author and illustrator of *A Splendid Friend, Indeed*, a Theodor Seuss Geisel Honor Book; *Treasure*; *No Place for a Pig*; and *We Keep a Pig in the Parlor*. She lives in McDonough, New York.

BUS STOP

BUS STOP

Suzanne Bloom

BUS STOP

BUS STOP